Calico Cat's Year

written and illustrated by Donald Charles

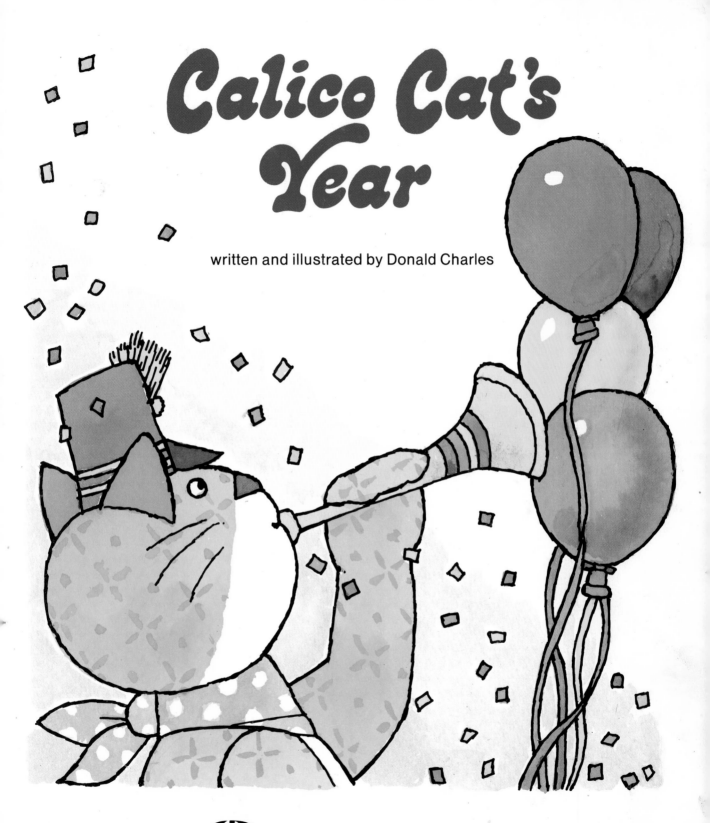

CHILDRENS PRESS, CHICAGO

For Jorde

Library of Congress Cataloging in Publication Data

Charles, Donald.
    Calico cat's year.

    Summary: Rhymed text and illustrations describe the
characteristics of each of the four seasons.
    [1.   Stories in rhyme.   2.   Seasons—Fiction]
I.   Title.
PZ8.3.C3833Cal   1984   [E]   83-23160
ISBN 0-516-03461-8

Calico Cat's Year

Calico Cat
loves the four seasons
of the year.

Now it's Spring, robins sing.

Kites fly
in the sky.

9

Rain showers bring flowers.

Summertime is
picnic time.

Swim, float,
sail a boat.

Catch a fish.
Make a wish.

In the Fall the leaves come down; red, yellow, orange, brown.

19

20

Rake the leaves,
pile them high.

Bake a plump, round
pumpkin pie.

23

Winter time is here,
we know, when we
see the ice and snow.

Skate, roll,
slide your sled.

When it's too cold,
stay snug in bed.

Calico Cat
knows the seasons
of the year. Do you?

= **Spring**

= **Summer**

= **Fall**

= **Winter**